Annie Flynn - first row, second desk

by Kevin Byrne

NEVER STOP NEVER QUIT

Portland, Oregon

NeverStopNeverQuit.com

Dedication

This book is dedicated to the staff and faculty of the Beaverton School District. Thank you for stimulating Eleanor's mind while keeping her body safe.

This story is published by NEVER STOP NEVER QUIT, a charitable organization whose mission is to raise funds, support treatment, and promote awareness in the fight against multiple sclerosis. One hundred percent of the profits from this book will go toward that fight.

Because it is a fight.
For approximately 2.8 million people
with MS worldwide, the fight is not over and it
won't be over until a cure is found.

It will never stop...nor will we
It will never quit...nor will we
This is why we fight!

Never Stop... Never Quit...®

Please visit NeverStopNeverQuit.com for more information about our organization, how we are giving back, and ways you can support our fight.

Thank you, Ellie – My Little Love.

Table of Contents

First Row, Second Desk

The second desk in the first row is prime real estate in every classroom. At least, that's how Annie Flynn saw it. Mrs. Grace's third-grade science class was no different.

Every room had five or six rows of desks, each with six. Overcrowding was common in urban elementary schools. Larger buildings, smaller class sizes, and more teachers were not possible due to a lack of funds. Annie didn't pay attention to any of it. She would be less distracted by restless children if she sat in the front, able to concentrate on the lesson at hand if she sat in the first row.

The second desk was perfectly centered between the teacher's desk and the activity board. The oak behemoths, classic pieces of Saxton Elementary's history, blocked your view if you sat one seat over to the right. There were distractions from the apathetic minions, playing games and passing notes, when you moved to the left. Annie adored her father's stories about the ideal location for navigating the obstructions, the same stories his father had told him. Annie agreed with Grandpa Flynn, of course. The second desk in the first row was ideal for studying.

The classroom doors at Saxton Elementary were usually in the back. That location met everyone's needs: teachers had three to five seconds to prepare for the next wave of students, those reluctant to enter and eager to leave had a direct line to the outside world, and Annie was able to stay focused on the lesson at hand.

Mrs. Grace arranged her science class to stand out. Her door was in the front. The window was covered over and painted black to match the surrounding walls. Her small, black-framed desk was in an area aptly named the void of space.

After a brief moment of disbelief upon seeing the unusual layout, eight-year-old Annie declared, "Old habits are hard to break," and claimed the first row's second desk. She decided there was no other place to be.

When Mrs. Grace closed the door, it proved to be Annie's saving grace, as it was the only way she was able to focus her attention on the lesson at all. As they extended out from both sides of the door, speckled constellations appeared to slowly cover the walls, increasing in intensity. Eighty-eight distinct patterns, each with a striking design and different number of stars. Annie had identified and named every one of those constellations by the time early April arrived.

Her favorite piece of trivia was the question about the thirteen signs of the zodiac. "But there are only twelve zodiac signs," was a teasing remark sure to spark debate.

"Dad! Don't be silly. I'm not talking about astrology; I'm talking about the zodiacal constellations. The number of constellations through which our sun appears to pass through each year is thirteen. That was something Mrs. Grace taught us back in September."

"As she did with me, dear," said Annie's dad. Mrs. Grace was old. "Do you recall their names?" "I'm sorry, but I can't." Another whimsical spark.

"Of course!" she replied. "Sagittarius, Capricornus, Aquarius, Pisces, Aries, Taurus, Gemini, Cancer, Leo, Virgo, Libra, Scorpius...and Ophiuchus."

"Bingo!"

The stars astounded Annie. Her ambition would be to visit every celestial body if it were possible. Unfortunately, the aspiring astronaut was never able to get away from the allure of the objects surrounding our own sun.

Mrs. Grace's speckling zoomed into the unique collection of bodies that make up our own solar system as she moved down the wall. Each planet, dwarf planet, and moon had its own set of characteristics, seemingly innumerable and incomprehensibly boring to every student. With the exception of Annie Flynn, every student.

Annie rushed to science class every afternoon to study the wall, skipping the last twenty minutes of lunch. Her hair bounced as she revisited all the bodies she had researched, memorized, and drafted into her dreams of a future with NASA. Her hair was dark as the starless door she would burst through.

When she is in orbit around the downgraded planet... ("How depressing.") Pluto, poor Pluto," she sighed.)

When she takes the first steps of humanity on Mars...

When her crew arrives on our moon for the first time...

Annie was finally brought back to Earth on that day, after spending over seven months in space. She took a position in front of the intricately painted orb, which was positioned to evenly divide our planet between the side and back walls. Annie was straining to remember new terms.

She kept repeating, "Oblate spheroid."

"Oblate spheroid," she struggled to say, varying her pitch and inflection to come up with the right sound.

"Oblate..."

It was pointless. Annie was drawn to her future in space once more. She took three steps sideways and came to a halt in front of Mars. Her hand raked the surface of the wall. Annie's fingers, which were manicured with pastel nail polish, painted bunny ears, and dirt, imagined an orbital path that began on Mars' solar face. Only her index finger remained when she finally settled in the upper corner of a dark, occluded mass after three trips around the planet, each time pulling one finger off the glide path. "The Syrtis Major Planum's northeastern region. That'll be my landing spot." Annie's voice was barely audible, but it never cracked, her volume was not soft, and her words were not made up. Annie Flynn stated it with the same zeal as she would for the rest of her life.

A flood of boys and girls broke the solitude of space with the click of the door handle. Annie's session was put on hold for the time being due to talk of a game of tag, the new cool book bag Sofie received for her birthday, and plans for afternoon ice cream. Her head hung low for a brief moment. Then her heart skipped a beat at the prospect of the next 45 minutes: science class.

As the flood of children subsided, Mrs. Grace appeared. "All right, please take your seats. In our limited time together, we have a lot to accomplish today." The scene was always the same.

"Scotty, please take a seat. Let's put our phones away for the time being. Everyone is aware of the rules. Lunch has come to an end. Scotty, you have your own seat!" Mrs. Grace waited another twenty seconds for the shenanigans to end with a frustrated but loving smile.

"Good afternoon, everyone," she said from the left of her desk, not from behind. Annie immediately strained forward and then leaned to the side, making sure her butt was firmly planted in the seat. Her efforts were in vain; she couldn't read anything on the large manila envelope held by her teacher. The rest of the class soon followed suit.

Mrs. Grace was deafeningly quiet as thirty-two pairs of eyes locked on her, then on the envelope in her hands, and then back on her. Thirty-one eyes shifted to Annie when she raised her hand. Despite seeing everything, the teacher teased them by remaining silent for her twenty seconds of retaliation.

"Yes, Annie," I say. "Do you have a question?" says the narrator. When Mrs. Grace finally spoke, everyone breathed a sigh of relief.

"I do, Mrs. Grace," I say. "Can you tell me what's in the envelope you're holding?" Proper, respectful, yet exuding the unmistakable charm that only a small child on the verge of bursting with curiosity can.

"Oh, this?" says the speaker. "This is a NASA letter." Andrew Woods, who had a crush on Annie, once hit her in the chest with the dodgeball in gym class, sending her sprawling back hard onto her back. Annie was equally taken aback by her teacher's announcement.

Mrs. Grace took a single sheet of paper from the envelope, unfolded it, and started reading. Annie felt a surge of energy from her toes to the top of her head with every word. "The letter is dated Wednesday, April 2," says the writer. She read the following:

Dr. James B. Garvin, NASA Goddard Space Flight Center

Chief Scientist, National Aeronautics and Space Administration

Mars Program Planning Group

Mrs. Margaret Grace and the Saxton Elementary School third-grade science class, Saxton, Ohio

There were a lot of happy guffaws. Annie reached out and gently tapped Stephanie Koritz on the shoulder. "That's the guy we wrote to before Christmas," says the narrator. Who else remembers what they did the day before the holiday break at school?

Thank you for your letter detailing your space exploration this school year, junior astronauts, scientists, and engineers. Your efforts inspire us at NASA, and we eagerly await the day when some of you will join our team.

Annie drew the attention of thirty-two pairs of eyes. "Yep," she said with a look in her eyes and a nod of her head. Mrs. Grace smiled briefly before going on.

Unfortunately, my Mars Program Planning Group is unable to wait for you to complete the eighteen to twenty-five years of education, training, and experience required to be considered for one of our first manned missions to Mars. As a result, on May 28, retired Air Force Colonel Marcus Cerro, the chief scientist for the Mars Surface Soil Analysis team, will visit your class. Mrs. Grace and our administrative staff will work out the details of the visit.

Colonel Cerro served as a mission specialist on five space shuttle flights, including Endeavor and Atlantis, as well as two separate Soyuz-launched missions to the International Space Station, in addition to assessing the viability of human colonization of Mars. He is looking forward to his first visit to the lovely town of Saxton, where he will be staying at the home of his Air Force Academy classmate Edward Flynn.

Thank you once again for your outreach and your unwavering commitment to assisting humanity in expanding its horizons.

Respectfully,

Garvin, Jim

There was no one in the room who responded. Mrs. Grace looked around, thinking about how their study—her efforts to connect the majesty painted on the walls to the children's future—had affected them. The final pushes were a letter, a promise, and a reference to a little girl's grandfather. This had become a reality.

All of a sudden, there's an eruption. Mrs. Grace was named the Best Teacher of All Time. Annie's celebrity shifted from her academic brilliance to her now-famous grandfather. She responded, "Yeah, but he only flew helicopters," downplaying it in the same way she downplayed any attention directed at her.

The class then gathered around Mars, who was projected on the back wall. Mrs. Grace let Annie lead the way as she walked through the physical characteristics that had already been mapped, pointing out where Colonel Garvin's team had taken samples and where they/she would first step down from the lander.

Only Annie Flynn noticed the click of the door handle coming from the void of space because the excitement was so loud...

The Greatest Summer of Her Life

The Greatest Summer of Her Life

The Greatest Summer of Her Life

The Greatest Summer of Her Life

The Greatest Summer of Her Life

The Greatest Summer of Her Life

Cadet Flynn

Cadet Flynn

Cadet Flynn

Cadet Flynn

Cadet Flynn

Cadet Flynn

Cadet Flynn

Cadet Flynn

Cadet Flynn

Lieutenant Flynn

Lieutenant Flynn

Lieutenant Flynn

Lieutenant Flynn

Lieutenant Flynn

Lieutenant Flynn

Lieutenant Flynn

.

Lieutenant Flynn

Lieutenant Flynn

Doctor Flynn

Doctor Flynn

Doctor Flynn

Doctor Flynn

Doctor Flynn

Doctor Flynn

Doctor Flynn

Doctor Flynn

Wife and Mother

Wife and Mother

Wife and Mother

Wife and Mother

Wife and Mother

Wife and Mother

Wife and Mother

Wife and Mother

Wife and Mother

Wife and Mother

Wife and Mother

NASA

NASA

NASA

NASA

NASA

NASA

NASA

NASA

NASA

NASA

NASA

NASA

NASA

NASA

NASA

The Red Planet

The Red Planet

The Red Planet

The Red Planet

The Red Planet

The Red Planet

The Red Planet

The Red Planet

The Red Planet

The Red Planet

The Red Planet

The Red Planet

The Red Planet

The Red Planet

The Red Planet

The Red Planet

Grandmother

Grandmother

Grandmother

Grandmother

Grandmother

Grandmother

Grandmother

Grandmother

Memorial

I never knew Annie Flynn when she was a child. We were supposed to have dinner together on the same day as the Saxton Elementary School massacre. Edward was going to pick me up at the airport, then drive me to Max and Carol's. I remember Carol when she was her daughter's age and if Annie was anything like her, I have a pretty good idea of the kind of girl Annie was. Still, on that horrid spring afternoon, I lost the chance to know Annie as a kid.

During the last few days, I spent quite a bit of time with the Flynn family. I learned so much about Annie—her dreams and her joys. I spoke with her classmates and friends. I marveled at the stories her teachers shared with me. Maggie, Mrs. Grace, walked me through the bloodstained classroom. She told me about Annie's passion: Mars. She was not the only one to talk about Annie's fascination with Mars. Only eight years old, yet she knew exactly what her calling in life was. I pulled out a folded piece of paper and reread the personal note Annie had attached to her class letter to Dr. Garvin. Everyone I spoke with confirmed what I myself had envisioned after I first read that letter.

I didn't know Annie Flynn as a child, but I know the woman she became in a world where school shootings don't extinguish a child's future. My job is—my whole career has been—identifying and interpreting potential in people. Our country's space program, and the people I have been entrusted to serve, rely heavily on the accuracy of my analyses. Let me describe to you who Annie Flynn became.

Saxton holds a bounty of dreams and memories for Annie. After a magical childhood, including the greatest summer of her life, she followed in her Grandpa Ed's footsteps and joined the United States Air Force Academy. In fact, Annie graduated as part of her grandfather's fifty-year affiliation class. Retired Lieutenant Colonel Flynn once again donned his blues and pinned second lieutenant bars on one shoulder of her uniform. Carol pinned them on the other.

Was she a pilot? Was she a doctor? It didn't matter. NASA was looking for, and found, the gem needed for their manned expeditionary mission to the surface of Mars. With a polished military career and the support of her husband and children, Colonel Annie Flynn took that long-awaited first step onto the surface of the northeastern region of Syrtis Major Planum. Thirty years before that, my team had determined the landing location would be optimal for her voyage someday.

Like her Grandpa Ed, Annie was gloriously proud of her accomplishments while serving. However, and I've seen the same reaction with four generations of Flynns, nothing compared to the joy she felt when surrounded by her children and grandchildren. Her legacy carried on beyond our own planet, while she and her offspring flourished forever right here in Saxton.

When an astronaut bursts beyond the surly confines of our humble orb, they are presented medals with words like "Exploration" and "Humankind" embossed on them. For soldiers, and airmen, and Marines who save lives when they alert their team to drop to the ground before a blaze of bullets strike, they are awarded posthumous medals inscribed with words like "Sacrifice" and "Valor." When an eight-year-old girl is taken from us, words like "tragedy" and "senseless" are freely tossed around, yet they are not permanently etched upon anything. In fact, those words are meaningless, as are those who use them only to promote selfish objectives. Annie's legacy was and will be different.

God be with you on your journey, Annie Flynn.

Marcus Cerro

Legacy

Four days after the massacre at Saxton Elementary, funeral services were held for the victims. It was the twelfth school shooting in the United States so far that year. In the first service, grieving family, friends, students and teachers gathered to say a final goodbye to eight-year-old Annie Flynn. At the request of her parents, to avoid what they referred to as the "disgraceful circus," news crews were denied entry to St. Michael the Triumphant church during the service. Many state and local politicians attended—they were asked not to contact anyone in the extended Flynn family.

Following the shooting, there were promises of "real" gun violence reform, especially from leaders from the bipartisan state of Ohio. Words like "tragic" and "senseless" were part of the language in proposed legislation. Fiery debates and riotous protests ensued.

One hundred and fifty-eight years later, a full five generations past its original target date, the Migrant IV module landed on the surface of Mars, in the northeastern region of Syrtis Major Planum. Twenty-three astronauts had died during the previous failed attempts.

Astronaut Dustin Zane stepped out of his spacecraft and onto the surface of the Red Planet. Without a sound, he knelt and thrust a brass plaque hard into the rocky soil. Embossed on its face was: "ANNIE FLYNN – SACRIFICE – VALOR – HUMANKIND."

Eighty-nine students were killed in school shootings that year.

About the Author

Kevin was born and raised in the Bronx, New York. A graduate of the United States Military Academy at West Point, he was diagnosed with multiple sclerosis (MS) in 1999 while commanding a US Army Air Cavalry Troop overseas. He is now medically retired and lives in Portland, Oregon, with his daughter, Eleanor.

Kevin devotes much of his time and energy toward overcoming the challenges of his own MS so that he can fight for others. He began writing and blogging in 2010 for the Department of Veterans Affairs, the National MS Society, and then NEVER STOP NEVER QUIT, a charitable organization he co-formed to expand his fundraising and advocacy in the fight against MS.

"...fantastic stories, where I'm limited only by my imagination, not by the confines of this stupid disease."

NMSS Leadership Conference
Denver, CO
November 2016

Copyright

www.ingramcontent.com/pod-product-compliance
Lightning Source LLC
Chambersburg PA
CBHW071233170626
46809CB00008BA/3030